I love God;
I love words;
I love God's words.

Monster-Sized Faith
Sinclair ©2017

Clan Sinclair motto, origins to 1068 a.d.

ISBN 13: 978-0-9916159-8-8
ISBN 10: 0-9916159-8-0

Library of Congress Catalog Card Number: pending

Sinclair Publishing
P.O. Box 2052
Rancho Cordova, CA 95741-2052

All persons contained within this book are fictitious, excluding Biblical references to God and Jesus. Any resemblance to any persons, either living or dead, is entirely coincidental. <u>No Bigfeet, Vampires, or Changelings were harmed in the writing of this book.</u>

Monster-Sized Faith
Sinclair ©2017

MONSTER-SIZED

Loretta Sinclair
Sinclair Publishing ©2017
Lori@SinclairInkSpot.com

Monster-Sized Faith
Sinclair ©2017

Finally, be strong in the Lord and in His mighty power. Put on the full armor of God, so that you can take your stand against the devil's schemes. For our struggle is not against flesh and blood, but against the rulers, against the authorities, against the powers of this dark world and against the spiritual forces of evil in the heavenly realm. (Ephesians 6:10-18)

Monster-Sized Faith
Sinclair ©2017

Monster-Sized Faith
Sinclair ©2017

Monster-Sized Faith
You can love both God, and your Imagination!

Bigfoot – Is It Real?

Changelings – Can people change?

Dragons – Are they good or evil?

Mummies – The Curse of the Mummy

Nessie – Is it Possible?

Shapeshifters – Did God Shift to Man?

Vampires – The Blood of the Dead

Witches – Are you a Good Witch or a Bad Witch?

Werewolves – Half man, Half Raging Beast

Zombies – The Walking Dead™

What can we learn about God from these myths and legends?

Come with me on a journey of faith and imagination. ~Lori

Monster-Sized Faith
Sinclair ©2017

Bigfoot

A very large, hairy, humanoid creature reputed to inhabit wilderness areas of the U.S. and Canada, especially the Pacific Northwest; also called Sasquatch.

Are You a Bigfoot Skeptic or Believer?

No one has ever caught a Bigfoot. Footprints have been found. Fuzzy videos are on TV. They have been seen only from a distance. Many sightings have been proven fake. This makes it even harder for true believers to be heard and understood. Each person has the right to make their own decisions on the subject. Sometimes we can be swayed by the opinions of others, but in the end, it is our choice to believe or not. So, is Bigfoot real?

Thomas, one of Christ's apostles has been given the name Doubting Thomas. When rumors of Christ's resurrection began to spread, he said the now-famous words:

"Unless I see the nail marks in his hands and put my finger where the nails were, and put my hand into his side, I will not believe." (John 20:25)

Jesus granted Thomas this wish. He appeared to all the disciples after His death and resurrection. To Thomas specifically He said:

"Put your finger here; see my hands. Reach out your hand and put it into my side. Stop doubting and believe." (John 20:26-27)

Thomas' response?

"My Lord and my God!" (John 20-28)

People have never really seen a Bigfoot, and yet believe.

But many people have seen the risen Lord, and still countless others refuse to believe.

What do you believe?

Bigfoot Has… Big Feet

Duh, you say, but stay with me on this one. This is important.

Bigfoot is what science calls a 'bipedal'. That means he can walk upright like a human. The term 'biped' means two legs. So, Bigfoot is on his two big feet all day.

The theory of evolution, (which I do not accept) would have us believe that creatures develop the attributes that they would need to survive. If you need eyes, then you magically develop eyes over a period of a few million years. I prefer to believe that a loving God gives us what we need without having to wait a few millennia to get it. That means that because Bigfoot is so large—nine to twelve feet by some accounts—he would need very large feet to balance, run, climb, and do all the things that Bigfeet need to do on a daily basis. My conclusion here, is that he would have very sore feet. Big feet, bearing big weight, would have big pain.

In Jesus day, people were on their feet all day too. There were few other modes of transportation. There was an occasional mule, or pack animal, but for the most part people would walk—all day, every day. They had sore, dirty, dry, cracked, aching feet. A woman came into the home where Jesus and the disciples were resting. She poured expensive perfumed oil on His feet, and dried them with her hair.

Then Mary took about a pint of pure nard, an expensive perfume; she poured it on Jesus' feet and wiped

his feet with her hair. And the house was filled with the
fragrance of the perfume. (John 12:3)

The disciples criticized her. Jesus told them to leave her alone. They felt the expensive perfume could have been sold to feed the poor—and they were right. But at that very moment, it was better used to soothe the aching feet of the one that would give His life for her. She cried at His feet, and He comforted her pain. She tended His aching feet, and He tended her aching heart.

That's a God of love.

Bigfeet With Big Feet

We established that Bigfeet have big feet. Whether you are a creationist or an evolutionist, the reason is the same. The size of the feet are in direct proportion to the weight that the creature carries. The pain that those feet feel is also proportionate to their size and weight. The more weight you carry, the more sore your feet will feel at the end of the day—or the end of your life.

At the last supper, Jesus knelt and washed the feet of His disciples. It was the Passover. The time right before Christ was betrayed and executed. He called his disciples together for one last meal, and a few last words of encouragement before the world would be plunged into the darkness of His death. And He washed their feet.

Now picture this. It was typically the job of the servants, or slaves of any household to wash the feet of the master and his guests. And here we have the Master, the teacher, the Messiah kneeling to wash the feet of His followers. Jesus knew how much their feet were hurting, and how much more their hearts would hurt in the coming days.

He came to Simon Peter, who said to him, "Lord, are you going to wash my feet?"

Jesus replied, "You do not realize now what I am doing, but later you will understand."

"No," said Peter, "you shall never wash my feet."

Jesus answered, "Unless I wash you, you have no part with me."

"Then, Lord," Simon Peter replied, "not just my feet but my hands and my head as well!" (John 13:1)

It was important for the disciples to understand that Jesus came to serve, not to be served. And by taking on the tasks of a servant, He demonstrated this personally.

Just like with Bigfoot, the pain in Christ's feet was in direct proportion of the weight that they carried. Jesus was about to carry the weight of the world—the sins of the entire world, past, present, and future—on His shoulders, and His feet. And at this most crucial moment the world has ever known, He thought of others before Himself.

That's My God!

Hiding in Plain Sight

Where does Bigfoot live? People claim to have seen them, but no one has ever found one. They have to be hiding somewhere. They are elusive creatures to be sure. Research tells us that they are concentrated in the Pacific Northwest region of the United States, Alaska, and southern Canada. Some have been reported in other regions of Canada, and in Russia. Other variations, such as the Yeti are reported in the Himalayas as well.

There are actual reports of people claiming that Bigfeet hide in and around the trees. In fact, there could be one in your backyard right now. They hide in plain sight. We can look for them all we want, but will never find them. Bigfeet find us, when they are ready. And apparently, they are not ready.

This is not the way God is. If you look around this world there is evidence of His beautiful creation everywhere. No, a person will not walk up to you, shake your hand, and tell you that He is God. He doesn't hide behind trees. But if that were to happen, then we would not need faith.

For since the creation of the world God's invisible qualities— his eternal power and divine nature—have been clearly seen, being understood from what has been made, so that people are without excuse. (Romans 1:20)

Look at the way this world is so intricately put together. We are just far enough away from the sun to create and sustain life. Any closer and we would burn up, and any farther away we would freeze. We have the perfect mix of oxygen and other atmospheric gasses to breathe. We have four distinct seasons, food, shelter, and everything that we need to survive. The earth spins on its axis perfectly and revolves around the sun in a perfect arc every single time. We can count on day and night, hot and cold, light and dark. Time is accurate down to the millisecond.

Bigfoot is afraid of people. He does not want to be seen or found. This is not so with God. He is not hiding. He walked with Adam and Eve in the Garden. He sent His Son to personally be with us here on earth. He is right here in plain sight. We just need to be willing to look.

Bigfoot Notes:

Changelings

(In folklore) an ugly, stupid, or strange child left by fairies in place of a pretty, charming child. A child surreptitiously or unintentionally substituted for another.

What is a Changeling?

Legend tells us that it is an entity that can shift into something or someone else. Lore says, it is the offspring of a fairy, troll, or an elf. It is most often left in the place of a sick child. The fairies then take the sick child to heal it where it will live forever with the fairy folk. In some cases, elderly people could be swapped for a changeling - someone to take their place and remove them from their suffering.

So where did this idea come from? I think I know.

Christ was sent to this earth to take away our suffering. He took our place on the cross. He has the power to heal the sick, and take away pain. The 'changeling' child gets all of the blame for everything that is wrong. So did Christ.

She will give birth to a son, and you are to give him the name Jesus, because he will save his people from their sins." (Matthew 1:21)

He was sent here as an infant. He had a purpose for coming. To take our place for the punishment we all deserve. We are the sick and broken children. He changed the future for us all. Because of Him, we can all live together in Heaven, the place where the sick and dying believers are taken where there will be no more tears or sorrow.

Monster-Sized Faith
Sinclair ©2017

If you look deep enough, myth and fantasy are not so far-fetched after all. For the answers, we need look no farther than the Bible, our source for all truth.

Do changelings really exist?

The One who served as absolute inspiration for this myth does.

Changelings – The Wicked Trolls

A changeling is a creature that is evil at heart. In legend, the changeling takes the place of an infant or a small child from a good family, and this troublemaking, evil child-like creature is left in its place. Legend tells that trolls from the underworld would creep into the homes and take the unbaptized children and leave their own offspring to be raised by the humans. They could not touch a baptized child because it was considered part of the church—claimed by God. Baptism is a blessing and sacrament that even evil recognizes and stays away from.

If you subtract the trolls and the changelings, the rest has Biblical truth in it. Once baptized, we are claimed by God, and sealed by the Holy Spirit. It is an outward sign to the world of the inner commitment we have made to Christ and the church. We are a being that now belongs to God. No matter what happens to us here on this earth, nothing can separate us from the Love of God.

Neither height nor depth, nor anything else in all creation, will be able to separate us from the love of God that is in Christ Jesus our Lord. (Romans 8:30)

Whoever believes and is baptized will be saved, but whoever does not believe will be condemned. (Mark 16:16)

Even the trolls know the truth!

Changeling Children

Sadly, many infants and very young children were accused of being changelings. This was due primarily to illness or deformity. If a child had seizures, was ill, mentally deficient, Down Syndrome, suffered from a bad temper, or was otherwise different, it was often killed. These precious children were innocent of anything other than just being what they were born to be.

In the Bible, there was also a large number of helpless children killed. It has become known as the Slaughter of the Innocents. You see, Herod the Great had heard that a new King – the King of the Jews had come. He was born under a certain star, and was going to save His people. This frightened Herod so much he ordered the death of all male children born during that time. Many thousands of innocent baby boys lost their lives needlessly. They were falsely accused, and died for it – just like those accused of being changelings.

When Herod realized that he had been outwitted by the Magi, he was furious, and he gave orders to kill all the boys in Bethlehem and its vicinity who were two years old and under, in accordance with the time he had learned from the Magi. (Matthew 2:16)

So too was Christ falsely accused. He died for no reason, having committed no crime. No one could honestly stand and give testimony for any wrongs He committed—although false witnesses did. Pontius Pilate's wife was so afraid after a dream she'd had that she begged her husband to have nothing to do with Him. She asked her husband to let Him go. History records what happened next.

Those who had arrested Jesus took him to Caiaphas the high priest, where the teachers of the law and the elders had assembled. (Matthew 26:57)

This is where He stood trial. This was the beginning of the end of Christ's time on earth, and the beginning of His reign as Savior.

So the next time you are falsely accused of something, remember the company you stand in. And thank God that we have a Savior that took our sins away. We can stand tall knowing that He went through the same thing, and still stands up for us today!

Why did the Fairies Take Your Baby?

The fairies are the culprits. They are the ones that allegedly stole human children and left the changelings in their place. Why would they do this? It has been said that the children that were taken were ill or deformed in some way. They were cursed. In other words, not normal.

All parents want 'normal' children. We want perfect families, perfect cars, perfect toys, perfect jobs, and perfect lives. When one of these things does not happen, it often causes stress and hardship.

Imagine living many hundreds of years ago, in a place where there was medieval healthcare, uneducated people, superstitions running rampant, and an enormous fear of the unknown. Anything that you did not understand was 'evil' and the devil was hiding around every corner. Then along comes a defenseless child born deformed. The first thought was that the poor thing was cursed. The myth of the changeling was a way to battle the evil they felt they were bombarded with. After all, a deformed or sick child couldn't be the parent's fault. They had to find a way to lay blame somewhere else.

The Bible teaches that we will not have perfect lives here on earth.

"I have told you these things, so that in me you may have peace. In this world, you will have trouble. But take heart! I have overcome the world." (John 16:33)

We do not have to blame our troubles and situations on anyone or anything else. We do not need to live in fear the way the people of old did. Something as simple as an illness or a deformity does not need to be a fearful or life-threatening event. Christ has overcome the world. Yes, we will have troubles here. But the reward of heaven is so much greater than anything we will ever face in this life.

Take Heart. God has everything in control, including all the trouble we can ever have.

Changeling Notes:

Dragons

A mythical monster generally represented as a huge, winged reptile with crested head and enormous claws and teeth, and often spouting fire. A huge serpent or snake.

Dragon Blood Makes Good Armor

I didn't realize that dragon blood could save your life. Legend tells that a single drop of dragon blood touching human skin can transform it into a thick, plate-like armor that will protect that person from all harm.

The problems presented with this are:

- Where to find a dragon;
- How to get a drop of its blood without getting killed;
- Is the armor permanent, or does it need to be refreshed?
- If it is permanent, how do I deal with a lifetime of plate armor for skin?
- Can I feel anyone or anything touch me?
- What are the side-effects?
- What will others think of me?

The good news is we don't need to rely on fabled dragon's blood. There is another type of invincible armor that we have at our disposal. The armor of God.

Finally, be strong in the Lord and in his mighty power. Put on the full armor of God, so that you can take your stand against the devil's schemes. For our struggle is not against flesh and blood, but against the rulers, against the authorities, against the

*powers of this dark world and against the spiritual forces of evil
in the heavenly realms. (Ephesians 6:10-18)*

The search is over. We don't need to worry about where to
find God's armor. It is in the Bible. We do not need to struggle
with where to find God Himself. He is everywhere. We don't
need to get a drop of Christ's blood. He has already shed it
freely for us. And His armor, is both permanent and eternal.

What armor do you wear?

Monster-Sized Faith
Sinclair ©2017

Is Your Dragon Good or Evil?

In some cultures dragons are considered good luck, and in other cultures, they are to be feared.

Let's consider the options.

Dragons are close relatives of the dinosaurs. They are reptilian in nature, and some kinds can also fly, making them related to the birds. Again, the theory evolution would want us to believe birds are just flying reptiles. My belief is that God created all living things, as they are, and for His purposes.

Another name for reptiles is serpents.

Serpents, predominantly across all cultures, are considered to be bad. Most people are born with an innate fear of snakes.

Now the serpent was more crafty than any of the wild animals the Lord God had made. He said to the woman, "Did God really say, 'You must not eat from any tree in the garden'?" The woman said to the serpent, "We may eat fruit from the trees in the garden, but God did say, 'You must not eat fruit from the tree that is in the middle of the garden, and you must not touch it, or you will die.'" (Genesis 3)

It was this one incident that led to the fall of mankind into sin. The serpent lied to Eve and told her that God was not telling the truth. He told her to eat the fruit, and that she would be as smart as God. She was tricked, and the rest—as they say—is history.

So, the beginnings of the serpent were not so humble. We are taught to beware, and for good reason.

Slayer of Dragons

In most every dragon movie or book, there is a dragon slayer. One man whose single purpose in life is to fight the evil dragon and save the world. This hero is willing to do whatever it takes, including sacrificing his own life, in order to save the village, country, or maiden... whatever is at stake. The only thing that matters to the hero is other people and saving them. He does not do it for fame or money, although some of this is typically either offered or given. He does it for his deep love of others and a desire for a better life for them. If it is the maiden he is saving, then there is often a wedding at the end, and he becomes the bridegroom for the one that he saved. They marry and live happily ever after—until another dragon returns for revenge.

All of this is based on truth and history. In our world the dragon is the devil and sin is evil. We were misled in the garden by the serpent—the great dragon—and fell into a world of sin. Our dragon slayer is Christ. He came for one purpose—to save mankind from eternal death. He was willing to do this solely for the love of mankind. He gave everything, up to, and including His own life to save us from evil.

The Apostle's Creed states our Christian belief like this:

I believe in God, the Father Almighty, maker of heaven and earth.

And in Jesus Christ, His only Son, our Lord, who was conceived by the Holy Spirit, born of the virgin Mary, suffered under Pontius Pilate, was crucified, died and was buried. He _descended into hell._ The third day He rose again from the dead. He ascended into heaven and sits at the right hand of God the Father Almighty. From thence He will come to judge the living and the dead. I believe in the Holy Spirit, the holy Christian Church, the communion of saints, the forgiveness of sins, the resurrection of the body, and the life everlasting. Amen.

When Christ descended into hell, he defeated both death and the devil. And in the end, He becomes the bridegroom to his faithful church. In this marriage of Savior and worshippers we truly can live happily ever after. This time it is for all eternity.

Christ is the only One who could have slayed sin and death. He conquered death for us—so we could spend eternity with Him.

The Woman and the Dragon

Then another sign appeared in heaven: an enormous red dragon with seven heads and ten horns and seven crowns on its heads. Its tail swept a third of the stars out of the sky and flung them to the earth.

Then war broke out in heaven. Michael and his angels fought against the dragon, and the dragon and his angels fought back. But he (the dragon) was not strong enough, and they lost their place in heaven. The great dragon was hurled down—that ancient serpent called the devil, or Satan, who leads the whole world astray. He was hurled to the earth, and his angels with him. (Revelation 12)

This is the beginning of what is called The Great Revelation. What we don't know is if this is a literal writing, or if it is figurative. Is the dragon a real dragon? Or is it representative of what the devil is and does? We don't know for sure. What we do know is that there will be a war between God and His loyal angels, and what is called 'the dragon' and those that were cast out of heaven with him. We do know that God will win, and believers will live for all eternity with Him. The dragon will be cast into the pit of fire known as hell forever.

Bible scholars will tell us that the dragon is the devil. He is red to represent the blood of the millions he has killed, and he is a dragon due to his fierce nature. The heads and the crowns represent various world governments that will be in power in the end

So, you ask me if dragons are real? Yes, at least one.

Dragon Notes:

Mummies

The dead body of a human being or animal preserved by the ancient Egyptian process or some similar method of embalming.

The Curse of the Mummy's Tomb

Tutankhamun was an Egyptian pharaoh who lived between roughly 1343 and 1323 B.C. He was known as the boy-king, taking the throne at the age of ten. By all accounts he was a good king. When he died, he was buried in an elaborate tomb with his many beloved things, and his slaves. Yes, during that time it was customary for the slaves, while still alive, to be sealed up in the tomb with their deceased masters. Mercifully, they were knocked unconscious first. They were left to die with the kings and queens that they faithfully served.

Legend tell us that many who open King Tut's tomb died. Now if we think about this rationally, an ancient tomb that was sealed for more than 2,000 years, with multiple deceased bodies in there, could have had some foreign bacteria, long dormant molds, or even viral cells released when the tomb was opened for the first time. These alone could have killed anyone not accustomed to them. But more than this, is one simple fact:

Everyone dies.

Is it a coincidence that they die when they are all around the tomb? Perhaps. Is it the curse of the mummy that so many want us to believe? No. But there is something else to consider too. We can start with the Ten Commandments:

"You must not make for yourself an idol of any kind, or an image of anything in the heavens or on the earth or in the sea. You must not bow down to them or worship them, for I, the Lord

*your God, am a jealous God who will not tolerate your affection
for any other gods. (Deuteronomy 5: 8-9 NLT)*

The ancient Egyptians were not Christian. They worshipped their own gods. By their own choice, they would not come under the protection of this commandment. I can only imagine that this would also be true for those chasing after these lesser gods as well, even today.

Jesus said, *"I am the way, the truth, and the Life. No one comes to the Father, except through Me." (John 14:6)*

This is one of my favorite verses in the Bible. *"I will bless a thousand generations of those who love me..." (Deuteronomy 5:10)*

Is there any more comforting thought than that?

Why Were the Mummies Entombed?

Ancient Egyptians believed that there was an afterlife, one very similar to this life. The reason that they packed their tombs with riches, possessions, and even their slaves was so that when they reached this afterlife, they would have all their valuables intact. Nice thought, but why do you think their tombs, filled with their valuable things, were there to be robbed? Because it didn't work. As one of my pastors used to say, "I've never seen a hearse with a U-Haul."™

The truth is there is only one way to an everlasting life after this one. That is through belief in Jesus Christ. He even proved this by raising one man from death. This is something no other religion has even been able to prove. They can make outrageous claims, but without proof, they are empty promises. Jesus proved what He could do.

Lazarus was Jesus' very dear friend, along with his two sisters, Mary and Martha. The sisters sent word to Jesus when Lazarus was sick. Jesus loved Lazarus, so they expected him to drop everything and come right away. But Jesus did not. He continued with his teaching and arrived at the small town after four days. He told the messengers that this sickness would not result in death, but to glorify God instead. When Jesus finally arrived, Lazarus had already been dead for several days. The sisters were upset. They told the Lord that if He had only been there, their brother could have been saved. Jesus cried over his friend. Then He went to the tomb and called him out. "Lazarus Come Out!"

And he did.

So they took away the stone. Then Jesus looked up and said, "Father, I thank you that you have heard me. I knew that you always hear me, but I said this for the benefit of the people standing here, that they may believe that you sent me."

When he had said this, Jesus called in a loud voice, "Lazarus, come out!" The dead man came out, his hands and feet wrapped with strips of linen, and a cloth around his face.

Jesus said to them, "Take off the grave clothes and let him go." (John 11 has the whole story).

Mummies do not have the ability to do this. Neither did Lazarus on his own. Mummy death is final and eternal. Only Jesus has the power to raise the dead to everlasting life.

Who are you following?

And why?

Mummies Do Not Decay

Through embalming, they are keeping their bodies in a form of suspense, so they will not be destroyed through natural decomposition. They want to keep both their bodies and their lives perfect for when the next life comes, or so they thought. We know now that mummifying is not the state of suspended perfection they thought it was.

The Bible promises us that we will be made perfect in heaven.

But the God of all grace, who hath called us unto his eternal glory by Christ Jesus, after that ye have suffered a while, make you perfect, establish, strengthen, and settle you. KJV (1 Peter 5:110)

We do not need to jump through a lot of hoops here on earth to earn our way to perfection, because we can never make it. Only God is perfect. Through belief in Him, our bodies will be made perfect when we enter Heaven. Only He can give us this gift.

Chasing perfection in this life, the way the ancients did, is not the answer. Mummification cannot bring afterlife perfection the way that belief in Christ can. Even through the process of mummification, and the hope to ward off decay, they are still in an eternal state of death.

Christ is the answer. He is the Way, the Truth, and the Life.

The book of the Dead

The Book of the Dead is an ancient Egyptian Funeral text filled with cursive hieroglyphs and color illustrations. It consists of a number of 'magic spells' intended to assist the dead person's journey through the underworld and into the afterlife. It was written by many Egyptian priests over a period of a thousand years.

The tradition of using the Book of the Dead involved their Pyramid and Coffin and other objects painted with the text the deceased would need. The mummy could use these written prayers to help them move from this world to the next.

Christianity has exactly the opposite.

The one who is victorious will, like them, be dressed in white. I will never blot out the name of that person from the Book of Life, but will acknowledge that name before my Father and his angels. (Rev. 3:5)

Unlike the Book of the Dead, the Book of Life is something that God keeps. It is not subject to erroneous additions or deletions. It is not something that can deteriorate or get lost. And it is not subject the temperaments of man. God alone chooses whose name is recorded. And that comes through belief in Jesus.

The Book of the Dead was a set of tests and questions that had to be said and passed to earn a place in paradise.

The Book of Life is a list of those people who have chosen to follow God—who have accepted Christ as their Lord.

One is seen as a ticket, if done correctly.

The other is a stamp of approval and guaranteed admittance. A sure thing.

Which book would you rather be in?

Mummy Notes:

Nessie

A large aquatic animal resembling a serpent or a plesiosaur-like reptile, reported to have been seen in the waters of Loch Ness, Scotland, but not proved to exist.

Nessie—Is it Real?

There are a great many believers in Nessie. Some think it is a he, others a she. Whichever, the creature has lived in the Loch (lake) Ness in southern Scotland for many centuries, according to legend. Some even believe that there is a whole group of these dinosaur-related creatures, not just one. Scientists have stated that the most likely option is that of the Plesiosaur.

For as many believers as there are worldwide, there are just as many non-believers, possibly more. They believe that it is a hoax, and is nothing more than a money-making venture for the locals. There couldn't possibly be a dinosaur leftover from that many centuries ago. After all, no one has ever seen it. Right?

After Christ's horrendous death on the cross, His body was buried in a borrowed tomb. Word got back to the Romans that the true Messiah would raise from the dead. The government was so afraid that someone would try to pull a hoax, they guarded the tomb.

Give the order for the tomb to be made secure until the third day. Otherwise, his disciples may come and steal the body and tell the people that he has been raised from the dead. This last deception will be worse than the first." (Matthew 27:64)

But the body was not stolen. Jesus was in fact raised from the dead. This was witnessed by many people, even up to 500 at one time. This did not stop the Roman authorities from trying to continue with their hoax theory. And to some degree it was successful. There were doubters then, and there are still doubters today. Some people still believe that Jesus' body was stolen and He was never raised from death to life, even though it has been witnessed and documented.

There is one big difference between the two events though. One has been seen, and one has not.

Christ was seen after rising from the dead multitudes. It was not an illusion like the Loch Ness monster. It was witnessed by many.

Do you believe it was a hoax?

I don't.

Nessie Possibilities

One theory says Nessie got trapped in Loch Ness during the time of a great flood, the barriers of the Loch were overflowed by the rapidly rising oceans, allowing a number of sea creatures to swim or drift into the Loch area. Then, after the flood waters swiftly receded, that left these sea creatures stranded behind in what is now known as Loch Ness.

Loch Ness is a very large lake, stretching over 23 miles long and 745 feet deep. It is easily possible for something very large to be caught in there, hidden for generations. Whether you believe in the monster or not, the theory is intriguing and certainly gives credence to the Great Flood of Biblical times.

The people of earth had become evil. This was something that God had never intended, though He knew it would happen. He spoke to Noah, the only righteous man at the time. God told him to build an ark. Then he was to take the animals, two of each kind, along with his family, and close themselves in it. When this was accomplished, God caused the world to flood. It rained for 40 days and 40 nights. The earth opened up, and the flood waters spilled upwards from deep below the surface, and the world flooded, killing all of the evil people.

Then, mankind got the chance to start again. We got a do-over. A second turn. A brand new start. And as a sign of His great promise never to flood the whole earth again, God gave us the rainbow.

Monster-Sized Faith
Sinclair ©2017

This symbol marks not only the beauty of the world after a rain, but the beauty and purity of God's promise. Nessie may or may not be real, but God's promise is. And His rainbow is our promise.

Forever.

Monster-Sized Faith
Sinclair ©2017

Nessie—Where is it?

Why can't we find her? Or him? We have the technology. We have sonar, depth finders, cameras, and underwater equipment. We can put a man on the moon, but can't find a giant swimming thing right here on our own planet. He/she can't go anywhere. Loch Ness is completely enclosed. It does not drain into the ocean. In fact, there is no ocean access at all. It is fed by some rivers and streams, but there is nowhere for Nessie to go.

I don't understand.

But then, there's a lot that I don't understand about our world. The Bible says not to worry about things that we can't understand. *In the end, all things will be made known. (Luke 12:2)* I used to think that meant things about our faith. How the disciples lived, what they experienced both before and after Christ died. How did the world really begin, one piece at a time. And things from history too, like the wars and conflicts between nations. But now I believe that it will be so much more.

When God says 'all things,' that literally means 'all things.' Everything that I don't understand will be included in there. Why did I go through all of the hurt and pain that I did? What is the reason I had to endure certain situations? And the biggest question of all: Why am I here?

That is one conversation I can't wait to have. That, and talking about Nessie.

Monster-Sized Faith
Sinclair ©2017

The Legend of the Loch

The Loch Ness monster first exploded on the scene in 1933 with what would become known as The Surgeon's Photo. Apparently, there was a big game hunter that came to find unknown creatures in the loch. He was exposed as a fake when the footprints that he found and sold photos to the news were imprints from a hippo footprint ashtray that he had collected. Shamed and disgraced, he found a different way to concoct a monster. He enlisted the help of a surgeon friend of his. This friend had an impeccable reputation, and a bent for practical jokes. They created the now famous photo of Nessie with a plastic dinosaur head and a submarine. And so, a legend was born.

There are many new religions and ways to 'find happiness' that have popped up in this century. And like the Loch Ness monster, most, if not all, leave us searching for something that is not there. A fake. An illusion. Something concocted by man to fool everyone who sees it. You are left continually searching for something that was never there in the first place.

There is only one way to the truth that will set us all free. Jesus the Christ. He and He alone is the Way, the Truth, and the Life. Through Him all men can be saved.

So, if my choice is to chase something that someone made up for their own gain and fame, or to go to the real thing... I'll take the real thing. Jesus.

Nessie Notes:

Shapeshifters

In mythology, folklore and speculative fiction, shapeshifting, or metamorphosis is the ability of an entity to physically transform into another being or form. This is usually achieved through an inherent faculty of a mythological creature, divine intervention, or the use of magic spells or talismans.

Shapeshifters

Creatures with the ability to change from one entity to another. This differs from the werewolf which can only change from wolf to human, and back again. Shapeshifters have many more choices at their fingertips, and are not limited to the stages of the moon to do so.

Tales of the shapeshifters date back to the middle ages. These creatures have an inherent ability to shift on command, or can sometimes use witchcraft to change. They can change into another species altogether, or in their more unscrupulous nature, they can change into someone or something that you recognize and love – perhaps a loved one, or a family pet. This way they are allowed into your personal surroundings to spy on you, or worse. They can also change into plants or objects, all the while retaining their supernatural abilities and fooling everyone around them.

So where does the legend of the shapeshifter come from? And what truth can we learn from this legend? Let's look at the Bible.

Christ is the one and only Son of God. He descended from God to become man for our sake. But there's more.

The Bible describes what has been called the Transfiguration. Jesus took Peter, James, and John up a mountain with Him. And there, they witnessed a miracle. They watched the Lord change. His face shone like the sun, and His clothes became as white as the light that enveloped Him. With Him came two other figures, Moses and Elijah. *(Matthew 17)*

Monster-Sized Faith
Sinclair ©2017

Peter, nervous and afraid, wanted to put up shelters for the three figures. But then a bright cloud enveloped them and they heard a voice. *"This is my Son, whom I love; with him I am well pleased. Listen to him!" (Matthew 17:5)*

How scary! They all fell to the ground, but Jesus came to them and told them to get up. He also instructed them to tell no one of what they had seen, until He had risen from the dead. Of course, they did not yet understand what that meant.

Can people change into potted plants and their dogs? Of course not.

Did Jesus change from God into a man? Not really. You see, He was already fully God, and fully man at the same time. Our human minds can't completely comprehend this. When we get to Heaven we will be able to see how, and why.

My job right now is to just believe.

So Why Do Shapeshifters Do What They Do?

Why do they shift? Because they want something. And depending on the movie you watch, or the book you read, it can be either for evil or for good. Mostly evil, in my own movie-watching experience.

Shifters need secrecy. They do not announce to the world what they are about to do, or why. They hide in the shadows, unseen by their unsuspecting victims. There are no witnesses to this shifting. That would ruin their evil plans.

The light shines in the darkness, and the darkness can never extinguish it. (John 1:5)

For we are not fighting against flesh-and-blood enemies, but against evil rulers and authorities of the unseen world, against mighty powers in this dark world, and against evil spirits in the heavenly places. (Ephesians 6:12)

But we do not need to fear. Light shines on the godly, and joy on those whose hearts are right. (Psalm 97:11)

You see, God knows what happens both in the dark and in the light. So, let the shifters stay in the dark. For one day the Light of Christ will overcome all the darkness, and all of the evil within it.

I'll stay in the Light of Christ. It's safe there.

Shapeshifters

Is it possible for something to miraculously change into something else? Can something old become something new? Something broken become perfect?

Shifters change into what they need to be. If a human form does not fit their needs, they become a tiger, or a bird—whatever meets the need of the moment. Their new shape is better. It is the perfect shape for what they need to accomplish at that exact moment.

The Bible tells us that this world will come to an end. There will be a terrible battle called Armageddon, and the world will be destroyed. But then there will be a new world.

"See, I will create new heavens and a new earth. The former things will not be remembered, nor will they come to mind." (Isaiah 65:17)

It will be created again and will be made perfect. Somehow God, through His miraculous ways will create a new perfect world. He will change this broken world into something beautiful and new. Things will shift, for the better.

God has the power to make things new and perfect. God has the power to shift things around in our world to meet our needs. God gave His only Son Jesus the power over our lives and our eternity. He can shift us from sinners to redeemed souls forever.

This is my blood of the covenant, which is poured out for many for the forgiveness of sins. (Matthew 26:28)
Have you shifted for Him?

Shapeshifters—New Creatures

In mythology, folklore, and speculative fiction, shapeshifting (or metamorphosis) is the ability of a being or creature to completely transform its physical form or shape. This is usually achieved through an inherent ability of a mythological creature, <u>divine intervention</u>, or the use of magic.

Think about it. The absolute ability to change from one thing into another. From a flawed and broken creature, into something perfect and brand new. The ability to discard the bad, and embrace the new. The ability to change.

Christ gave us this ability at His resurrection. We have become new creatures in Him. When we accept Him into our lives, He discards the bad, and changes us from the inside out. He morphs us into His own image, and gives us a new identity in Him. We are sealed by His blood, and marked by His own hand. We are truly changed forever.

Therefore, if anyone is in Christ, the new creation has come. The old has gone, the new is here! (2 Corinthians 5:17)

Shapeshifters transform the body. Christ transforms the soul.

And Christ's transformations are eternal.

Shapeshifter Notes:

Vampires

An unnatural being, commonly believed to be a reanimated corpse, that is said to suck the blood of sleeping persons at night. In Eastern European folklore, a corpse, animated by an undeparted soul or demon, that periodically leaves the grave and disturbs the living, until it is exhumed and impaled or burned.

Monster-Sized Faith
Sinclair ©2017

Vampires and Jesus

The world has been obsessed with vampires for centuries. From the medieval folks who feared them and dug up newly buried corpses to re-kill them—to the legends of Hollywood— vampires thrill and capture our imaginations. But where did this legend come from really?

By now we all know that they are not real, except in our minds. They are the living legends of old. Vampires have an eternal existence. I hesitate to call it 'life' since it is no life at all. They drink the blood of another living thing—animals or people—for their strength and survival. They come out in the dark, because they are darkness itself. The sacrifice of the intended victim is what keeps them alive.

Now to the Bible. At the Last Supper Jesus held up a loaf of bread and said, *"take and eat. This is my body, broken for you for the forgiveness of sin. Do this in remembrance of me."* Then he held up a glass of wine to his disciples and said, *"take and drink. This is my blood shed for you, for the forgiveness of sin. Do this in remembrance of me." (Matthew 26:28).* We do this as a reminder of the great sacrifice He made for us, so that we could have eternal life. True life, not just existence. The sacrifice of one man is what keeps us all alive. We must never let the world forget.

I think that the legend of the vampire is meant to throw people off the one true Savior. I think that this was a ploy of the enemy (one of many) to lead people the wrong way. We need to be strong and reject what is not true. We see it in popular culture all the time, but we need to keep in mind what the true meaning of eternal life is, and what the blood sacrifice really means.

Enjoy the movies and books, always remembering the true Blood of the Covenant with Jesus Christ, the Son of God. His blood alone can give eternal life.

Movies are entertainment.

God is life.

Creatures of the Night

Vampires are creatures of the night. Depending on which legend you listen to, or which movie you watch, they cannot bear the sunlight. They might sparkle, die, or just melt back into the darkness. Some will burn up in sunlight. They sleep in coffins, because they are that close to death. Vampires are repelled by garlic. (That one I still have trouble figuring out). They cannot stand crucifixes, are burned by silver, and can only die with a stake through the heart. Often, when a suspected vampire was killed, he would have to be re-killed over, and over again, just to make sure.

The Bible tells us that sin hides in the darkness. Just like cockroaches, if you shine the light of Christ into a dark situation, the darkness will flee – along with everything in it. Light and dark cannot occupy the same place. It must be one or the other. The Light of Christ is stronger than any darkness that the world or its enemies can produce.

Imagine being in the darkest place that exists, like a deep cave. A place so dark that you cannot see your hand in front of your face. Now light a match. Invite the light in, and what happens? The darkness completely disappears—at the speed of light.

There is no fear in love. But perfect love drives out fear, because fear has to do with punishment. The one who fears is not made perfect in love. (1 John 4:18)

Monster-Sized Faith
Sinclair ©2017

So, the next time that fear invades your life – whether it is real or imagined, invite the Light of Christ to chase away the darkness. When His presence shows up, nothing evil can stand against it. And the best part, is we need only to ask. The simple words, "Jesus I need you" are enough. I love that. And I love God.

Share this with your vampire-loving friends. Invite them into the light of Christ with you.

How Do You Cure a Vampire?

There is no known cure for vampirism. Once you are bitten by the undead (according to legend) then you become the undead for all eternity. We all know how to kill them, a stake to the heart. They hate silver. Garlic repels them. They shy away from crucifixes and burn in sunlight. Doomed for all eternity in this life of darkness and nothing. Day after day hunting, seeking to drink the blood of other living things just to stay in an eternal state of existence. They hunger for their soul's nourishment.

But they are drinking the wrong kind of blood. It is not human blood, or animal blood that can save them. They need the blood of the Covenant, the Lifesaving blood of Jesus Christ to live forever.

On the night in which He was betrayed, at the Last Supper, Jesus made it clear why He was willingly going to His death for all mankind—although no one understood it at the time. He told the disciples that He would shed His blood for the redemption of all, and by instituting the practice of the Holy Communion, we could reaffirm this promise until His return. Some churches believe that this is a representation of His blood, while others believe that a miracle happens each time the grape juice or wine is prayed over and it is the actual blood of Jesus in the communion cup. Either way, the act of taking communion is the washing away of your sins, and re-affirming Christ's sovereignty until He returns to claim us all. It is obedience and worship.

So the next time you run into a vampire at a costume party or on Halloween, you will have a story to tell. Lead them to the blood that can save them and give them an eternal life, not just an eternal existence. Invite them to come and try the true Blood of the Covenant.

Jesus said, "I have come so that you may have life, and life abundant." (John 10:10)

True life.

I've Seen Them! They're Real!

People swear they have seen vampires. That is why they believe in them.

We've seen them in the movies for sure. Medieval people swore they saw them walking around at night. Every Halloween they appear in various forms at parties and for Trick-or-Treating. There are groups of people who actually believe that they are literally vampires, and drink each other's blood. We have seen them. They are real. We believe.

Jesus was crucified. That is a fact. He was guilty of no crime. Also a fact. And He rose from the dead. This is not fiction. Not myth or folklore. He was seen.

Many people saw Jesus after his death, the first being Mary Magdalene. He spoke to her and asked her why she was crying. They conversed.

He was seen by fishermen, and regular people. The Bible says He was seen by "the masses" detailing out multiple sightings of everyday people, and once at a gathering of over 500.

He appeared to the disciples multiple times, once behind a locked door. They were afraid for their own lives and feared persecution after Christ's death. Thomas, nicknamed Doubting Thomas *said "I will believe it when I see Him and can put my hand in His wounds."* So Jesus went to him and said *"Here I am. Put your finger in my wounds. (John 20:27)"*

Yet still the masses do not believe. Myth, legend and lore, like vampires are more believable to some, than the One who rose from the dead - and proved it! Many, many people saw him. He spoke to them, touched them, encouraged and comforted them. There was an empty tomb, and the large stone had been rolled away. These are all documented facts, witnessed by countless people.

He told them "You believe because you have seen. Blessed are those who have not seen and still believe." (John 20:29)

I believe. Do you?

Look at the facts, and then decide.

Vampire Notes:

Werewolves

In folklore and superstition, a human being who has changed into a wolf, or is capable of assuming the form of a wolf, while retaining human intelligence during the full moon cycles.

Monster-Sized Faith
Sinclair ©2017

Super Human Strength of the Werewolf

I love dogs. Cats are okay, but my true loves are always the dogs. (Don't tell my cat, Princess. She'll never forgive me.) For me, the breed that is the closest to a werewolf is the German Shepherd. They have a thick mane of gorgeous fur that you can really run your fingers through, and an elongated snout showing vicious looking canine teeth that they seldom choose to use.

Werewolves are known to have thick fur, and superhuman strength. When transformed by the full moon they are not completely animal, but still retain some human qualities, one of which is choice. They can choose when to attack and when to stand back. While they do not always have the choice of being a werewolf, they have free will to some degree while under the moon's influence.

In the movies, the werewolf is always betrayed by those close to them. Someone finds out what they really are, gossip starts, and the wolf is hunted, often killed. They had to keep their condition a secret. No one could ever know.

There is a similar story in the Bible I am reminded of - The story of Samson. He had beautiful sleek hair and superhuman strength. His enemies tried to tame him, but they could not. He could not be beaten. Once when the townspeople tried to trap him, he tore the doors and posts of the city gate off and carried them to the hills. Samson was strong. He could snap bowstrings easily. But there was a secret.

Samson's downfall was he fell in love with the wrong person. He was betrayed. Delilah persuaded him to give up his secret. She pretended to love him, and he trusted her. He had been dedicated to God at birth. He could not touch the dead, or consume fermented drinks. But the most noticeable part of the vow was that no razor had ever touched his head. One day while he was sleeping, she had his enemies come and cut his hair off. His vow with God broken, he instantly lost his strength (as the werewolf does when he returns to human form). He was captured, enslaved, and tortured. They gouged his eyes out.

But his hair started to grow back. Then he prayed. His strength returned. When he was tied between two pillars at the temple of his enemies' god. Samson asked his God for renewed strength. He used his great power to pull down the pillars and crush his enemies. Samson died that day, but so did more of his enemies than he had killed during the earlier part of his life. *(Judges 16)*

Werewolves have enemies, just like people do. It seems like there is always someone trying to take us down. But be strong, even superhuman strong. God can answer your prayers when you need it.

He did for Samson.

The Curse of the Werewolf

So where did the first werewolf come from? Legend tell us that the werewolf first came to life in the late 1500's during the witch trials in eastern Europe. The wolf was a cursed man, whom the witches hated, and so they cursed him. This man then continued to curse others, through scratches or bites, as well as other witch curses on more people.

The first cursed man was Cain, from the book of Genesis. You see, there were two brothers. Cain and Abel. Abel worked the flocks and Cain, the fields. Cain was the oldest, yet Abel found favor with the Lord. Abel always brought the best of his flock for his offering, while Cain brought some of his crops. The Lord favored Abel, and not Cain. This angered Cain greatly. His heart burned with jealousy and rage. He killed his brother in the fields, and then tried to hide it.

Now Cain said to his brother Abel, "Let's go out to the field." While they were in the field, Cain attacked his brother Abel and killed him. (Genesis 4:8)

For his punishment, Cain was banished from the rest of his family, and his fields. He was cursed to forever work the fields, but they would barely produce for him. And when Cain voiced his fear of being killed by others, God marked him so that others would leave him alone. He could live in his misery and work hard for the rest of his days. He was cursed to be a restless wanderer.

This all sounds familiar with the same legend of the werewolf. Could it be that those creating the werewolf stories also read the Bible? The similarities are striking, but the lessons are the same.

God curses those that disobey Him and break His laws.

I sure don't want that to ever be me!

Being a Werewolf is Immortal

Legend says the first werewolf survived over 800 years with no food or water, in a state of hibernation. They descend from the 5th century and are <u>presumed</u> extinct. They can be killed by other creatures, or humans, but left to themselves, they do not age or die. They have piercing cobalt eyes, and froth at the mouth as though rabid. Upon changing, they grow (morph) into a creature of a much greater size, thereby ripping off all their clothes as they grow. This does not matter because they have their thick fur to cover their bodies. After turning, they become truly terrifying creatures, howling at the moon that haunts them, and terrorizing those around them with their aggression.

There is a story in the Bible, of two men. They lived in a place called Gadarenes, in the tombs. Today we would call that a graveyard, but at the time it was a series of caves that people used for burial. These two men had wild eyes, wild unkept hair, and ran around with no clothes on. They howled at the moon, terrorized the locals, and could not be near anyone or anything without destroying it. These were violent men. Everyone in the town was afraid of them. Had the term werewolf been around back then, it is possible these two men would have been labeled as them. However, there was another explanation. *(Matthew 8:28).* Demons.

Jesus was visiting the area. When He approached them, something interesting happened. The demons that had been possessing them became frightened, and spoke.

Monster-Sized Faith
Sinclair ©2017

"What do you want with us, Son of God?" they shouted. "Have you come here to torture us before the appointed time?" (Matthew 8:29)

The demons acknowledged that Jesus was the Son of God, and that there is an appointed time where they will be held accountable. Interesting. Even the devil knows there will be an end to his antics.

The demons begged Jesus not to kill them, but to allow them to go into a herd of pigs (about 2,000) and He did. The pigs all went crazy, started running, ran off a cliff, fell into a lake and drowned. The two men were healed. But the townspeople were so afraid of what they had seen they begged Jesus to leave. He did. (Matthew 8:31-32)

Nothing else is mentioned about the two men, and how their lives went on after that. Were they reunited with their families? Did they become believers? I sure would want to follow the One who had saved me.

So, what can heal a werewolf?

Clearly, the Word of God.

Monster-Sized Faith
Sinclair ©2017

The Legend of the Werewolf

Half man, half raging beast; unable to control his actions and desires. Left to the mercy of—of what? The full moon? Where did this legend come from?

Man has always struggled with his darker side. From the fall of Adam and Eve in the Garden of Eden, sin temps us all. And all, except One, has fallen prey. It is always a choice with us.

Now many will say that their sin is not their fault. Like the werewolf, they had no choice. They were at the mercy of the elements that control them (the way they were raised, or being provoked), and therefore are not responsible for their actions. Like the werewolf is at the mercy of the full moon, so we are at the mercy of evil. But the truth is we are all responsible for our actions. We can choose our good side over our bad side. God will never give us more than we can bear.

No temptation has overtaken you except what is common to mankind. And God is faithful; he will not let you be tempted beyond what you can bear. But when you are tempted, he will also provide a way out so that you can endure it. (1 Corinthians 10:13)

Are werewolves real? Well, I've never seen one, although I love to read about them. Because I can relate to the inner conflict they suffer. I think we all can—from wanting to do the right thing, but constantly being pulled away, to the joy they feel when they come back to their true selves. The reconciliation they face with friends and loved ones, in some ways mimics the reconciliation we have with Christ when we realize the depth of our own sin and come back to Him.

Is the struggle of the werewolf real? Yes. As real as the struggles you and I face every day.

So next time you read about, hear, or even see a werewolf, remember this: There is evil in the world, but through Christ we can overcome. Evil does not have to rule our lives. We have the choice to turn to Him.

"For everyone who does evil hates the Light, and does not come to the Light for fear that his deeds will be exposed. (John 3:20)

For I do not do the good I want to do, but the evil I do not want to do--this I keep on doing. (Romans 7:19)

Werewolf Notes:

Witches

A person, now especially a woman, who professes or is supposed to practice magic or sorcery; a sorceress. A woman who is supposed to have evil or wicked magical powers.

Monster-Sized Faith
Sinclair ©2017

Are You a Good Witch or a Bad Witch?

This line was made famous in the movie <u>The Wizard of Oz</u>™

I was standing in line at the grocery store recently and overheard a conversation between the store clerk and the customer ahead of me. The clerk was telling the customer that she was a witch, but she was a white witch, that means a good witch. Good witches do no harm. They are in tune with the environment, and completely connected with Mother Earth. I forget how often her coven met, but they were all there to support each other and keep them in line with their main mission.

Except, one previous customer had made her mad about something so she had to put a hex on her. ('Had to'— she said).

Now I personally believe that the only 'power' we have is what was given to us by God. The Bible speaks of witches, and also warns people to stay away from anything resembling witchcraft. It does not differentiate between good witchcraft and bad witchcraft. I believe that because of our sinful nature, we are not always able to make good decisions. Have you ever made a bad decision while trying to do something good?

Exactly.

Let no one be found among you who sacrifices their son or daughter in the fire, who practices divination or sorcery, interprets omens, or engages in witchcraft. (Deuteronomy 18:10)

The fact is that our sinful human nature renders us unreliable. We can try our best, and still fail. There are certain things that God instructs us to stay away from for our own good. Witchcraft is one of them. In this, we need to be obedient, and follow God's word. For our own good.

He always has our best interests at heart.

What is the Difference Between Magic and a Miracle?

One is from God, and the other is from man. One is a blessing, and the other is a curse.

God sent Moses to Pharaoh to deliver a message. *"Let My people go."* Pharaoh did not listen. *(Exodus 8:1)*

The Lord said to Moses and Aaron, "When Pharaoh says to you, 'Perform a miracle,' then say to Aaron, 'Take your staff and throw it down before Pharaoh,' and it will become a snake." *(Exodus 7:9)*

So, Moses and Aaron went to Pharaoh and did just as the Lord commanded. Aaron threw his staff down in front of Pharaoh and his officials, and it became a snake. Pharaoh then summoned wise men and sorcerers, and the Egyptian magicians also did the same things by their secret arts: Each one threw down his staff and it became a snake. But Aaron's staff swallowed up their staffs. Yet Pharaoh's heart became hard and he would not listen to them, just as the Lord had said. (Exodus 7:12)

Moses and Aaron were both part of the miracle. They did not perform the miracle. It was not within their power to perform. Aaron did what he was instructed to do by the Lord, but Pharaoh responded with magic. He responded with what the Bible calls "secret arts" and the trick was performed by sorcerers. It was dark magic.

Sorcery and witchcraft are an affront to God. Instead of giving the glory and respect to God, people take that on themselves. Have you ever had someone take responsibility for something that you had done? Something you worked hard for, and created? Only to have that taken from you?

That's how God feels too. Let Him perform the miracles in your life.

Leave the cheap tricks to the devil.

The Salem Witch Trials

In Salem, Massachusetts, during the period from 1692 to 1693 there was a series of witch trials. Twenty people were executed, nineteen by hanging, and one by being crushing to death. Five others, including two infants died in prison. Twelve other women had previously been executed in the colony in years prior to these witch trials. It was the most notorious case of mass hysteria from the early colonial times in our country. Dozens more people were accused. Those accused were given a trial in front of the town magistrates. They were given the chance to confess, receive a punishment, and live. A special court had to be appointed, with judges being brought in from neighboring townships due to the sheer volume of accused being arrested and needing trial.

George Burroughs refused to confess to sorcery and witchcraft. To these deeply religious Puritans this false confession amounted to denying God. He lamented his innocence until tears came to the eyes of those listening. He then recited the Lord's Prayer—something that a true witch is supposedly unable to do. He then went to his death proclaiming the sovereignty of the Lord, and his own innocence.

But not all did. Many, when faced with their own executions, confessed to a crime they did not commit in order to live. They received a physical punishment (beatings or lashes) but were allowed to live. I've often wondered how they felt many years later in their lives, understanding the severity of what they had done. They denied God. We can look to the Bible for some understanding.

Then Jesus told them, "This very night you will all fall away on account of me, for it is written:

"'I will strike the shepherd,
and the sheep of the flock will be scattered."

But after I have risen, I will go ahead of you into Galilee."

Peter replied, "Even if all fall away on account of you, I never will."

"Truly I tell you," Jesus answered, "this very night, before the rooster crows, you will disown me three times."

But Peter declared, "Even if I have to die with you, I will never disown you." And all the other disciples said the same. (Matthew 26:31)

But after Jesus' arrest, while He was being beaten and tormented by his captors, *Peter watched trying to hide himself, and in fear of what was happening to his Lord.*

Now Peter was sitting out in the courtyard, and a servant girl came to him. "You also were with Jesus of Galilee," she said.

But he denied it before them all. "I don't know what you're talking about," he said. (Matthew 26:69)

Then he went out to the gateway, where another servant girl saw him and said to the people there, "This fellow was with Jesus of Nazareth."

He denied it again, with an oath: "I don't know the man!"

After a little while, those standing there went up to Peter and said, "Surely you are one of them; your accent gives you away."

Then he began to call down curses, and he swore to them, "I don't know the man!"

Immediately a rooster crowed. Then Peter remembered the word Jesus had spoken: "Before the rooster crows, you will disown me three times." And he went outside and wept bitterly. (Mark 14:72)

I can't help wondering if those accused witches who confessed to witchcraft when they were truly innocent felt the same way Peter did. Scared. Ashamed. Guilty.

The good news is that Peter was forgiven, and they would have been too, if they confessed that sin and sought forgiveness.

That's the wondrous and amazing love of God.

The Banshee – Witch of Death

There is an old Gaelic legend of the Banshee. Some describe her as an evil fairy, and others a witch. She appears out of nowhere, and heralds the death of a loved one with her shrieks in the darkness. Some Celts believed that she is wailing and mourning the death of someone already taken, while still others believed that it was a sign of an impending death. She is described as an old hag with disheveled hair that is either red, orange, or yellow in color. When several banshees appear in the darkness, it is to mark the passing of a very holy or spiritual person.

She is the witch of death.

Exodus 11: The Plague of the Firstborn

Moses carried the message from God, to the Pharaoh of Egypt. *"Let My people go."* Pharaoh refused, so God sent a series of plagues, announced in a message by Moses and Aaron to persuade Pharaoh to change his mind and release the enslaved Israelites. He did not. It was time for the last of the ten plagues, and what would come to be known as the Passover.

Moses told Pharaoh that the angel of death would be sent to claim every firstborn son in the land. This meant the firstborn of the Egyptians, of the slaves, and even the firstborn of the livestock in the fields.

There will be loud wailing throughout Egypt—worse than there has ever been or ever will be again. (Exodus 11:6)

But God made a distinction between Israel and Egypt. He told His chosen people, Israel, to slaughter a year-old male lamb without defect, and paint the blood over the door arch. That way the angel of death would pass over their home, and not harm their children.

This was the true angel of death, sent to a hard-hearted Pharaoh who refused to listen to the God of the Universe. He paid the price with his own firstborn son. The Banshee would surely have shrieked near his household.

Then, after losing his own firstborn son, Pharaoh let God's people go.

Witch Notes:

Zombies

The body of a dead person given the semblance of life, but mute and will-less, by a supernatural force, usually for some evil purpose.

Monster-Sized Faith
Sinclair ©2017

What is One Thing Common in all Zombie Movies?

Other than the zombies don't know that they're dead, it is the fact that there is always a loved one out looking for the dead person. They refuse to believe that they are dead until they see if for themselves. They still believe that there is both time, and a way to save the undead. If they just try hard enough, work long enough, sacrifice enough time, talent, and money, the zombie can be saved.

People that don't know Christ are like the zombies in the movies. They are the original walking dead. And we, their loved ones, are busy trying to talk, work, and sacrifice enough to save them. But the truth is that we cannot save another person. Only God can save them. We can encourage, pray, love, lead, and do whatever it takes to get the word of God out in front of them, but the choice to accept God's redemption is theirs, and theirs alone.

Jesus answered, "I am the way and the truth and the life. No one comes to the Father except through me. (John 14:6)

The truth is, for our loved ones, we should never give up on them. There is a cure for being the walking dead. And as long as they draw breath on this earth, there is still a chance. You never know when that right moment will be for someone, so never give up. Keep your light shining… for Christ. The light of the world.

Monster-Sized Faith
Sinclair ©2017

The Parable of the Persistent Widow (Luke 18)

Then Jesus told his disciples a parable to show them that they should always pray and not give up. He said: "In a certain town there was a judge who neither feared God nor cared what people thought. And there was a widow in that town who kept coming to him with the plea, 'Grant me justice against my adversary.'

"For some time he refused. But finally he said to himself, 'Even though I don't fear God or care what people think, yet because this widow keeps bothering me, I will see that she gets justice, so that she won't eventually come and attack me!'"

And the Lord said, "Listen to what the unjust judge says. And will not God bring about justice for his chosen ones, who cry out to him day and night? Will he keep putting them off? I tell you, he will see that they get justice, and quickly. However, when the Son of Man comes, will he find faith on the earth?" (Luke 18)

How Do You Kill a Zombie?

You cut its head off - at least according to the zombie movies. There are a great many tools to do this with too. There are zombie chainsaws (very messy), hammers, and claw looking things. The most effective seems to be a machete. Quick and painless (although I don't think that zombies can actually feel anything). It is also the least messy for the zombie-killer. You can lop its head off in a second.

We non-zombie humans also cannot live without a head - both literally and figuratively. Who knew? Have you ever heard the phrase, "Don't let it get to your head?' or, 'Don't get a big head about it?' That means don't go thinking that you are more important than anyone or anything else.

Here is what Paul tells us in 1 Corinthians:

Now if the foot should say, "Because I am not a hand, I do not belong to the body," it would not for that reason stop being part of the body. And if the ear should say, "Because I am not an eye, I do not belong to the body," it would not for that reason stop being part of the body. If the whole body were an eye, where would the sense of hearing be? If the whole body were an ear, where would the sense of smell be? But in fact, God has placed the parts in the body, every one of them, just as he wanted them to be. If they were all one part, where would the body be? As it is, there are many parts, but one body. The eye cannot say to the hand, "I don't need you!" And the head cannot say to the feet, "I don't need you!"… But God has put the body together, giving greater honor to the parts that lacked it, so that there should be no division in the body, but that its parts should have equal concern for each other. If one part suffers, every part suffers with it; if one part is honored, every part rejoices with it. (1 Corinthians 12:12-30)

So there you have it—what both humans and zombies have in common. We all need each other, and we all need to function together in order to be one body of Christ.

Zombie Apocalypse

The world seems to be filled with zombies these days, both literal and figurative. Last weekend my city hosted the Zombie Walk 5K run for charity. You start the run/walk, but at some point begin to be chased by a zombie (a person dressed as the undead). If you get caught, then you must drop out of the race. Only the ones who manage to stay away from the zombie attackers will win the prize.

Zombies have always been part of the fantasy/horror movie subculture. They are the attackers, coming to rob you of your life, feelings, and happiness. Today they are more mainstream. The Arts and Entertainment Channel (A&E)™ even created their own original series called <u>The Walking Dead</u>™. It was a huge success, and even has spin off series called <u>Fear The Walking Dead</u> (A&E)™.

So what does it really mean to be a *walking dead*? The Bible tells us that we are all dead without Christ. He is the only way to eternal life. Without Him we have no hope. We are true Zombies.

In Hell, there is eternal torment and suffering. There is no future, no rescue, and no hope. Just like the zombies that we see walking around on movie sets and fun runs, there is no feeling and no direction. They simply exist. I don't know about you, but that's not good enough for me. Eternal life has been handed to all of us, no strings attached.

...I have come that they may have life, and have it to the full. (John 10:10)

Don't settle for eternal death, when we have everlasting life waiting. All we need to do is confess our sin, and say yes to Jesus.

In the same way, count yourselves dead to sin but alive to God in Christ Jesus. (Romans 6:11)

Zombies; the Original <u>Walking Dead</u>™

Zombies are literally the walking dead. They have no soul, no conscious, and an appetite for killing the living, and eating their brains. They will literally suck the life right out of you if you let them. If they are going to be dead, they will bring as many others with them as they can. In election years (all puns intended) I think we may have a few running for public office!

All kidding aside, we, as a world are fascinated with this concept, and the thought that people can raise from the dead. Where does this all stem from?

I believe it is from Scripture. And we have documented proof. Look at the Bible, in *Matthew 27:50-53.* After Jesus rose from the dead, he was followed by many others (Holy people also raised), who made their presence known and were seen by many people. These were people who had died, and were literally brought back to life with Jesus. They were dead—really dead—and then they were up walking around again. BAM! The first reported Zombies. But this was different. When they were raised from the dead, they were raised back to eternal life. They were not empty walking shells turned into killing machines. Their bodies were perfect, as promised by God. Not the decomposed killing creatures in the movies. They had souls and brains. They were raised to get the reward for the Holy life they lived.

That's where I want to be—right by Jesus side when my time comes! You can too. Just believe.

Zombie Notes:

Coming soon:

<u>Legendary Faith</u> – Follow popular and urban legends
and see what we can learn about God from them.
©2017 Sinclair Publishing

Available Now: <u>The PriZin of Zin</u>: (both print and ebook)

Enter the realm of The PriZin of Zin. A fantasy world
of wonder and discovery. Find out what a Bigfoot, the
Loch Ness Monster, pirates, indians, and an Armed
Forces Corporal have in common. A story of growing
trust and faith in something greater than ourselves.

What is your prison? How far would you go for a
friend? When everything you know to be true about life
is turned on its head... When you have been tested
beyond your ability to cope... When everyone that has
called you 'friend' has fled in the face of danger... Who,
or what, will stand and fight? Either for you? Or against
you? Do you stand a chance of winning? Or will you
be...Chained: And dragged off to...The PriZin of Zin

Find us on <u>www.Amazon.com</u> ,
<u>www.BarnesAndNoble.com</u> , or <u>www.Kobo.com</u>

Monster-Sized Faith
Sinclair ©2017

Visit us at www.SinclairInkSpot.com or

www.Faith-And-Fantasy.com

Find me on Twitter @LorettaLea

And on my author page on Facebook,
https://www.facebook.com/Loretta-Sinclair-233166803490094/ and;

Sinclair Publishing
https://www.facebook.com/SinclairBooks/

God's peace be with all of you.

~Lori